This series is dedicated to my family, and all military families, for their unwavering support, their infinite love, and their sacrifice for our country.

- Johnathan Edmonds

www.mascotbooks.com

For more information, please contact:
Mascot Books
560 Herndon Parkway #120
Herndon, VA 20170
info@mascotbooks.com

Library of Congress Control Number: 2012952881

PRT0213A
ISBN-10: 1620861534
ISBN-13: 9781620861530

Printed in the United States

NAVY
SERVICE PALS ™
★ TRAVEL AROUND THE WORLD ★

JOHNATHAN EDMONDS

ILLUSTRATED BY
ADAM SCHARTUP

Tidy Tammy Tender raced into the port at Norfolk Naval Base in Virginia. "Hello, everyone. I have some exciting news!" she exclaimed.

Tidy Tammy delivered supplies to the bigger ships and always knew everything first. The Navy Service Pals gathered around Tidy Tammy, waiting to hear why she was so excited. There was Sneaky Sammy Sub. He was calm, silent, and usually stayed underwater. Above him was Handsome Holden Hornet, a small, sleek guy with two engines. Crazy Carl Cruzer was the risk-taker of the group. Steady Stacy Seahawk had a keen eye for spotting objects in the ocean. Finally, there was Crafty Christy Carrier, the leader and mother-figure of the group.

"What's going on?" asked Crazy Carl.

"Yes, please tell us your news," chimed in Crafty Christy.

"Well," said Tidy Tammy, "I just found out we are being transferred to San Diego Naval Base in California. Isn't that the most exciting news?"

The Service Pals didn't respond.

"What's wrong?" asked Tidy Tammy.

Crazy Carl spoke up, "How do we get there? We can't go across the country on roads like Jumping Jenny Jeep in the Army or Honorable Henry Humvee in the Marines. We can't fly there like Totin' Tony Tanker or Fast Freddie Falcon in the Air Force."

"But that's the best part!" exclaimed Tidy Tammy. "We get to sail all the way around the world to get there. Just think of all the places we'll get to see!"

"Will we get to see Europe?" asked Sneaky Sammy.

"What about Egypt?" asked Crazy Carl. "I've always wanted to see the pyramids."

Steady Stacy chimed in, "I would like to visit China and Australia."

Tidy Tammy answered, "We will get to see all those places and more!"

Crafty Christy noticed Handsome Holden remained quiet. "What's wrong, Handsome Holden?" she asked.

"I don't want to move," he said. "I don't have any friends in California."

"Don't worry, Handsome Holden," said Tidy Tammy. "The five of us are all going together and when we get to California, we'll make some new friends."

"Are you sure?" asked Handsome Holden.

"Of course," said Tidy Tammy. "It's easy to make friends when you move to a new base. Now, we've got to get ready for our trip because we leave in one week."

Everyone went to sleep excited that they were going on a voyage around the world. As they slept, their heads filled with dreams of what each place would be like.

As the week went by, word spread that the Navy Service Pals were going on a trip around the world. Totin' Tony and Fast Freddie flew in to see them off. Crafty Christy was nervous. She was in charge of leading the others around the world.

"Can I really do this? Can I lead them around the world?" Crafty Christy asked Totin' Tony.

"Don't worry, trust yourself," he responded.

A large crowd gathered at the port to say goodbye.

"Send me a postcard!" exclaimed a boy.

"Take a lot of pictures!" yelled a girl.

Nervously, Crafty Christy led them on their journey.

As they traveled through the night,
the sky lit up with many stars.

"It's so peaceful," said Sneaky Sammy.

"How many stars can you count?" asked Crazy Carl.
"One...two...three..."

Everyone was really enjoying their journey!

The next day, Crafty Christy woke up and noticed something floating in the water. "Everyone! Watch out for the iceberg!" It was a wonderful place, full of snow and polar bears.

"Where are we?" they wondered as they sailed by the iceberg. A quick check of the map showed they were near Greenland.

The group headed toward Europe. The next morning, they passed a beautiful green place with sheep and horses.

"We've finally made it to Europe! We're passing by Ireland right now! Look at the castles!" exclaimed Sneaky Sammy.

"I have always wanted to live in a castle," said Steady Stacy.

Next, they sailed by England. Tidy Tammy pointed out Stonehenge and Big Ben. Shortly after that, they could see the Eiffel Tower in France.

As they continued to sail along, it got warmer and then a strange animal with a hump appeared on shore.

"What is that?" asked Crazy Carl.

"I think it is a camel," Handsome Holden replied, "but what is that over there?"

"It's the Egyptian pyramids! They are so tall," said Tidy Tammy.

As they continued by Africa, they noticed many animals. "Look over there!" yelled Sneaky Sammy. "I see elephants and zebras! Wow! Is that a lion?"

They continued on to Australia where they saw lots of kangaroos. They passed the Great Barrier Reef. The water was so clear, they could see hundreds of fish swimming around the reef.

The Service Pals turned north and sailed toward China where they had a perfect view of the Great Wall. A short time later, they passed Japan.

"Wow, look at that mountain! It's so beautiful with all that snow on the top," said Steady Stacy.

"It's Mt. Fuji, the tallest mountain in Japan," replied Handsome Holden.

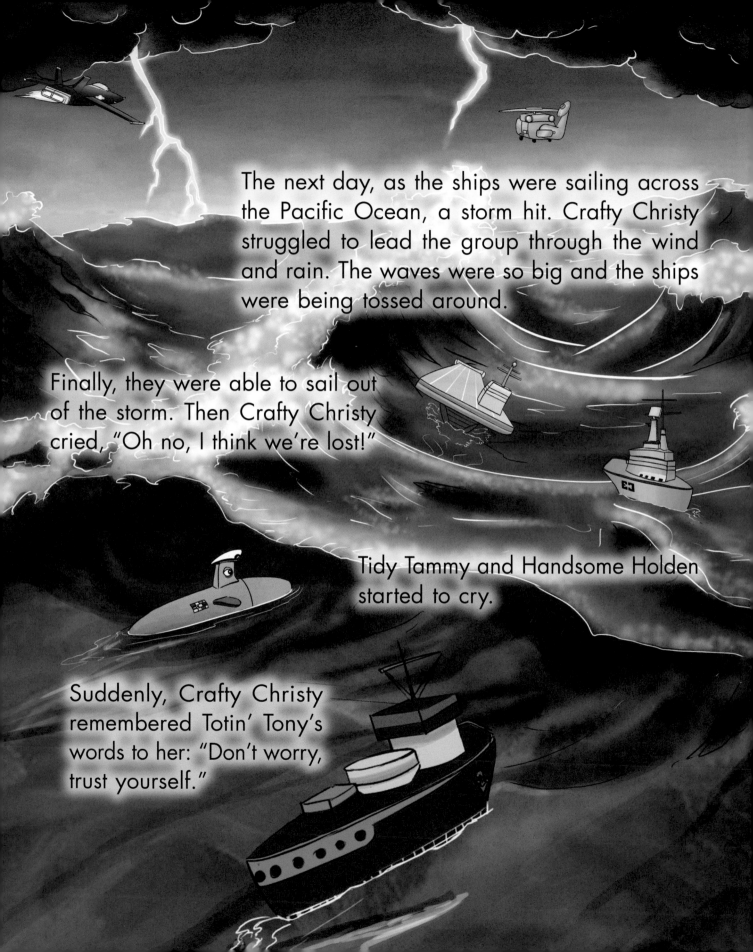

The next day, as the ships were sailing across the Pacific Ocean, a storm hit. Crafty Christy struggled to lead the group through the wind and rain. The waves were so big and the ships were being tossed around.

Finally, they were able to sail out of the storm. Then Crafty Christy cried, "Oh no, I think we're lost!"

Tidy Tammy and Handsome Holden started to cry.

Suddenly, Crafty Christy remembered Totin' Tony's words to her: "Don't worry, trust yourself."

She knew it was up to her to get the Service Pals safely to California so she took a deep breath and looked around. After a moment, Crafty Christy smiled; she knew where they were. "Don't cry, Tidy Tammy and Handsome Holden. I know just where we need to go. We will be in California tomorrow morning," she reassured them. "Follow me."

The next morning as the sun rose in the sky, the Service Pals could see the port at San Diego. They did it! As they got closer, they could hear the crowds cheering for their arrival.

"Full speed ahead!" exclaimed Crafty Christy.

"Look at all the people," Crazy Carl said. "I can't believe they are all here to welcome us."

Welcome to California!

As Crafty Christy led the Service Pals into the port, there were cheers of "Welcome to California!" and "We're so happy to have you here!"

When they finally docked, the children in the crowd immediately started climbing aboard to check out the new ships. Tidy Tammy and Handsome Holden looked at each other and smiled. They knew they were going to like California. It already felt like home.

THE END

Sneaky Sammy Sub is a submarine. He is silent when moving, can go underwater for over 30 days ▶ at a time, and can dive to a depth of over 800 feet.

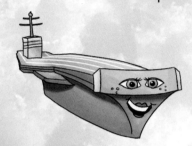

Crafty Christy Carrier is an aircraft carrier. ◀ She carries over 40 planes and 6,000 people. Her catapult can launch planes into the air.

Tidy Tammy Tender is a tender ship. She provides supplies to other ships including ▶ food, water, and electricity.

Crazy Carl Cruzer is a cruiser ship. He is built ◀ to protect the other ships from danger but can also handle the role of scouting for other ships. He is the second largest ship in the Navy.

Handsome Holden Hornet is a fighter jet. He can go very fast and has 2 engines. He ▶ usually has 1 pilot, but sometimes may have 2.

Steady Stacy Seahawk is a single rotor helicopter. ◀ Her primary role is to search and find lost people. However, she can also serve as medical and personnel transport and a fire fighter.

Hilarious Hank Hawkeye is a 2-engine turbo prop. He is also known as Super Fudd. He is a flying radar station used to find other ships and aircraft.

Tinkering Tommy Tomcat is an old fighter jet. He has 2 big engines and 2 aviators. His wings can move at high speeds and he is very maneuverable. He can fly at over 1,500 mph and can fly at an altitude of 50,000 feet.

Protective Paula Prowler is an old jet plane. She has 4 crew members and 2 jet engines. She is built for electronic surveillance and has a gold plated canopy.

Groovy Gary Greyhound is a transport plane with 2 turbo prop engines. He can carry 10,000 pounds over 1,000 miles. He has a large rear cargo ramp to load cargo quickly.

Hovering Hugo Hovercraft is a vehicle who can travel on water and land by floating on a cushion of air. He is powered by 2 engines and can reach a top speed of 40 mph fully loaded.

Friendly Fran Frigate is a slightly smaller ship than Crazy Carl who is responsible for finding submarines like Sneaky Sammy. She can also supply cargo to other ships.

COLLECT ALL OF THE BOOKS IN THE

SERIES

AIR FORCE SERVICE PALS IN THE AMAZING AIRSHOW

MARINE SERVICE PALS IN THE HONOR RELAY

ARMY SERVICE PALS SEARCH FOR SERGEANT MIKE

NAVY SERVICE PALS TRAVEL AROUND THE WORLD

ABOUT THE AUTHOR

Johnathan Edmonds, a sixteen-year veteran of the U.S. Navy and U.S. Air Force, grew up in Blain, Pennsylvania. At the age of eighteen, he enlisted in the U.S. Navy as an Aviation Electronics Technician. After being honorably discharged, he studied computer engineering at Virginia Tech. Upon receiving his Bachelor's degree, Johnathan began his computer engineering career and soon joined the U.S. Air Force Reserves, fulfilling his lifelong desire to fly planes. He also earned a Master's degree from NC State University in computer engineering. He resides with his family near Raleigh, North Carolina.

To learn more about Johnathan and the Service Pals, please visit www.myservicepals.com.